About this book:

This classic children's book follows a white bear's ingenious escape from two hunters, with the use of his magic pencil with which everything he draws becomes real. Children will love the way Bear draws himself quickly out of a very tricky situation.

BEAR HUNT

Anthony Browne

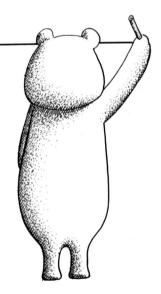

PUFFIN BOOKS

One day Bear went for a walk.

Two hunters were hunting.

They saw Bear.

Look out! Look out, Bear!

Quickly Bear began to draw.

Well done, Bear!

But there was another hunter.

Run, Bear, run!

Out came Bear's pencil.

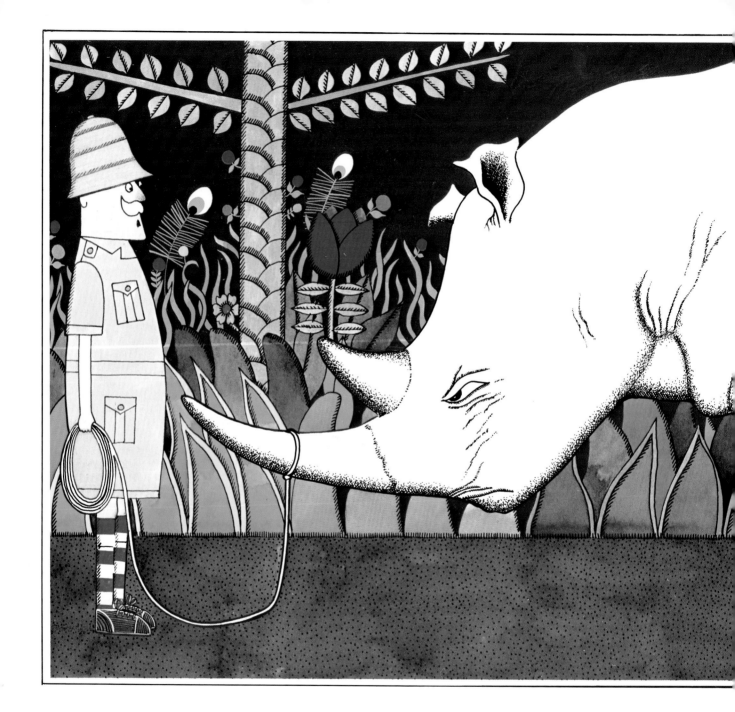

And Bear walked on.

Stop! The hunter's back . . .

Swiftly Bear got to work.

Look up, Bear!

Bear is caught.

But Bear still had his pencil . . .

Clever Bear!

HELP – !

Do something, Bear!

So Bear escaped . . .

. . . and the hunters were left far, far behind.

Also by Anthony Browne

KNOCK KNOCK, WHO'S THERE *(with Sally Grindley)*

Some other Puffin picture books

HAIRY MACLARY FROM DONALDSON'S DAIRY *Lynley Dodd*
MR ARCHIMEDES' BATH *Pamela Allen*
STARTING SCHOOL *Janet and Allan Ahlberg*

PUFFIN BOOKS

Published by the Penguin Group
Penguin Books Ltd, 80 Strand, London WC2R 0RL, England
Penguin Group (USA) Inc., 375 Hudson Street, New York, New York 10014, USA
Penguin Books (Canada), 90 Eglinton Avenue East, Suite 700, Toronto, Ontario, Canada M4V 2Y3
(a division of Pearson Penguin Canada Inc.)
Penguin Ireland, 25 St Stephen's Green, Dublin 2, Ireland (a division of Penguin Books Ltd)
Penguin Group (Australia), 250 Camberwell Road, Camberwell, Victoria 3124, Australia
(a division of Pearson Australia Group Pty Ltd)
Penguin Books India Pvt Ltd, 11 Community Centre, Panchsheel Park, New Delhi – 110 017, India
Penguin Group (NZ), cnr Airborne and Rosedale Roads, Albany, Auckland 1310, New Zealand
(a division of Pearson New Zealand Ltd)
Penguin Books (South Africa) (Pty) Ltd, 24 Sturdee Avenue, Rosebank, Johannesburg 2196, South Africa

Penguin Books Ltd, Registered Offices: 80 Strand, London WC2R 0RL, England

www.penguin.com

First published by Hamish Hamilton Ltd 1979
Published in Picture Puffins 1994
20 19 18

Copyright © Anthony Browne, 1979
All rights reserved

The moral right of the author/illustrator has been asserted

Made and printed in Italy by Printer Trento Srl

British Library Cataloguing in Publication Data
A CIP catalogue record for this book is available from the British Library

ISBN-13: 978-0-14055-356-7